T0206590

Drum City

Drum City

by Thea Guidone

Illustrations by Vanessa Newton

Dragonfly Books New York

Drum.

Drum.

Boy in the yard

drumming so hard,

calling all kids

to come drum in the yard.

Drum on some kettles and cans!

Here they come!

They run to the beat of the drum.

Drum.

Bowls and
buckets,
cartons
and cans,

barrels
and bins,

and pots
and pans,

mops on pails,

and rusty old rails—

a frolicking, rollicking ruckus of rumbling **drums.**

Drum.

Jump to the sound,
dance all around,

loud on the tubs and the
tins that they found.

"March!" calls the boy
in the yard full of drums,

hundreds and
hundreds of
drums.

Hum of the city.

Humdrum of the city. HO-hum.

15

Something is coming.
They watch and they wonder,

assuming the booming
is summertime thunder.

Thumping and **pounding**,
the echo resounding

the sound of the
pound of the **drums**.

Drum.

Buses and cabs,

bakers and cops,

people in **banks**,

people in shops,

everywhere, everything, everyone

STOPS

Wendy's Market
Fresh Fish
OPEN
The Freeman Bank
Uncle Will's House of Sweets
Robin Mitchell's Designs
SALE
TAXI

for **kids** marching in
with their
drums.

Drum.

People in traffic keeping the beat
on the **hood** and the trunk
and the bicycle seat.

Mamas in rollers
rock babies in strollers,

clapping and **stomp**ing and
stamping their feet to the

drums.

Drum.

Drums everywhere,
in the park, in the square,

by the pond with the ducks,
in the zoo with the bear.

From Hill Street to Main
to Sassafras Lane,

kids shake up
the city with
drums.

Bear's House
Bear
is very Smart and
Very, Very, Kind.
down what se
ery deep, or she fell ver
she went down
ried to look down and
to, but it was too
he sides of

Drum.

The **city** becomes a city of **drums**,
banging and clanging as **everyone** comes.

A **summer** parade, a drummer parade,
a magical bucket-and-bowl
serenade

in the heart
of a city of
drums.

Drum.

Up in the **planes**,
down at the docks,

bang on a lid or a crate
or a **box**.

Everyone jams.
Everyone
rocks.

Everyone,
beat on your
drum.

Drum.
Play hard, play soft,
play happy or blue.
You listen to me.
I listen to you.

Over the mountains
and over the **sea**,

drumming like you,
drumming like me.

Together we **drum**.

Let's

drum!

For kids in my family and kids in "The Group."
—T.G.

This is dedicated to my sister, my friend,
my 20/20 and my hilariously funny family.
Thank you JC, Ray, Coy, Will, Zoe, Ben, Chyna,
The Jeans, Loredan, Ms. I, and Dad.
Love y'all.
—V.N.

Text copyright © 2010 by Thea Guidone
Cover art and interior illustrations copyright © 2010 by Vanessa Newton
Design by Becky James

All rights reserved. Published in the United States by Dragonfly Books, an imprint of Random House Children's Books, a division of Random House LLC, a Penguin Random House Company, New York.
Originally published in hardcover in the United States by Tricycle Press in 2010.

Dragonfly Books with the colophon is a registered trademark of Random House LLC.

Visit us on the Web! randomhousekids.com

Educators and librarians, for a variety of teaching tools, visit us at RHTeachersLibrarians.com

The Library of Congress has cataloged the hardcover edition of this work as follows:
Guidone, Thea.
Drum city / by Thea Guidone; illustrations by Vanessa Newton. — 1st ed.
p. cm.
Summary: A young boy begins banging on pots and pans in his front yard, enticing other children to join him, and before long the entire city is feeling the beat.
[1. Stories in rhyme. 2. Drum—Fiction.] I. Newton, Vanessa, ill. II. Title.
PZ8.3.G948Dru 2010 [E]—dc22 2009031747

ISBN 978-1-58246-308-7 (trade) — ISBN 978-1-58246-348-3 (lib. bdg.) —
ISBN 978-0-553-52350-8 (pbk.) — ISBN 978-0-385-38730-9 (ebook)

MANUFACTURED IN CHINA
10 9 8 7
First Dragonfly Books Edition

Random House Children's Books supports the First Amendment
and celebrates the right to read